52 WEEKS 52 POETS

ANIRUDH KAUSHAL

FanatiXx Publication

AM/56, Basanti Colony, Rourkela 769012, Odisha
ISO 9001:2015 CERTIFIED
Website: *www.fanatixx.in*

"52 WEEKS 52 POETS"

By: **ANIRUDH KAUSHAL**

ISBN: 978-93-89557-15-2

English Poetry

1st Edition

BOOK FORMATTING: PHALGUNI JAGADEESH
BOOK COVER: SAGAR SAMAL
PRESENTED BY: REASONS AND LAUGHTER

DISCLAIMER

This is a work of fiction. Our editors have tried their best to edit the content of all the author/authors and check the plagiarism. All the write-ups in this book are unique and are only published in this book.

In case any plagiarism or error is found, the author is the sole responsible and not the publisher.

<u>ACKNOWLEDGMENT</u>

I would like to thank 'Reasons and Laughter' for providing me with such a glorious opportunity to work as the Compiler for my book. It took me 5 months to complete the job, which were filled with many lessons and I am thankful for each and every one of them. I hope to be constantly working with them.

I would also extend my gratitude towards my parents and friends who were constantly motivating me throughout the whole project and guided me in my quest.

Lastly, I would like to sincerely thank all the poets who willingly took part in the project and gave me the golden opportunity to read their lovely poetry and brought this dream of mine to life.

<u>Compiler</u>

Anirudh Kaushal, a ' Dead Poets Society' inspired poet who took ' The Captain' as his pen name to honour Mr. Keating. Weaves verses when he needs a moment to relax and finds peace in his movie collection ,Linkin Park, his diaries and plans to own a kennel one day.

FOUNDER

JAPNEET KAUR

Japneet Kaur, daughter of Mr. Surjeet Singh and Mrs. Dilpreet Kaur was brought up in Indirapuram, UP. She is pursuing German language and BA programming course from Delhi University. She is a passionate writer who loves to pen down her emotions and environment and strive to make her parents proud. She is even working on her very first novel making her one step closer to her goal.

Instgram : @sheedreamss

EDITOR

PHALGUNI JAGADEESH

""There are many ways to achieve something in life and knowing the purpose of living, I got mine through words."

She is from Tamil Nadu, she has completed her MBA in Marketing and HR. Writing was her hobby once upon a time which has become her profession now. She is a passionate writer who loves to ink her emotions without any flaws. She is a free verse writer and also has invented two of her own poetry forms. Reasons and Laughter has given her a great platform to explore, learn and improve herself in all possible ways.

Instagram : @phal_candy & @pjinklings

DESIGNER

SAGAR SAMAL

Sagar Samal is a Photographer, Image Manipulation and Colour Grading Artist.
Hardworking with a "Create Something Awesome" Mentality.
A graduate in Bachelor of Computer Application but an Artist By Heart.

Instagram : photosign.cf

JAPNEET KAUR

If a tomorrow comes!!

If a tomorrow comes when your fingers will search for
mine to fill the gaps of love and you don't find it
anymore,
When thine eyes will search for my ocean I see through,
to serve a drink and you don't find it anymore,
When your lips out of thirst will keep running in search
of mine and you won't find it anymore
When in search of me, you will try to figure out your
essence in every single letter of my poem and you won't
find it anymore
Those desolated streets you will walk in at the magical
hour hunting for just a single glance of mine and you
won't find it anymore,
At that moment you will not be able to find beauty in
the most beautiful thing,
The silence you alway wanted whenever i use to get on
your nerves will cut you deeper from inside,
When you will sit peacefully near the sea seeing it
turning into a beautiful scenery made by me, hanging
on the wall of your living room and again you would
keep staring for hours at the entrance hoping for me to
arrive till the time reality of my body turning into ashes
would slap you hard on your face and you would realise
that I am never going to show up at your entrance like I
used to do,
When you will try to hear the cackle of laughter in every
picture of mine, hanging on the walls of your empty
bedroom,
When every door of your house you pass by will screech
harder and harder for me to get back again piercing

your ears till it bleeds and you will search for me
everywhere in the house possible, hoping that I am
hiding from you to make you mad at me,
When you would want me to burn like a fire out of the
ashes and you would cry your heart out to get this off
your chest to let it go,
When my pieces
will scream at you telling tht I am incarcerate in every
inch of your holy skin and there is nowhere you could
find me except yourself,
At that time you would realise the love I had for you
since years and that, all the promises I made, the words
I spoke, the love I showered till the "time unknown" was
all true.
That very moment, you will find me incarnated within
you and that day you will fall in love with the poem of
my soul.
For the world I might be dead but you will always find
my presence inside yourself.

The 52 Poems

Srishti Nautiyal

The future tittered from behind its veil,
A sultry laughter that punctured the tranquility of
knowing.
I asked to see its face, it laughed again.
It couldn't talk, not yet; its ability to speak to me hadn't
developed.
The past brooded beside me,
Tugging at my sleeve, an impatient child who only
wanted me to spend time with it,
To relive what had been the good and the bad.
It had ramblers that wrapped around my arms and legs,
My mind; they only stopped their pulling when I stared
them down and named them.
The past wouldn't look at the future, couldn't stand the
lustrous enigma it concealed by its very presence.
But I wanted to know it and couldn't. It couldn't even
know itself.
The present was absent, its purred promises lingering
like smoke in a room without windows, without doors.
It was held on the air, a bird in takeoff, but never flying
away.
I was the present. In eternal still life, we battled with our
peace.
A peace we could only hold for a moment before it
slipped away, wind and water crumbling it, time and
space making it a memory.
There was no more solitude.

Only desire. To be found in triplicate: to heed the past,
to live the present, to know the future. There was no
more solitude.

Vanshika Aggrawal

<u>TEACHING...</u>

Everyone wants to look towards the sun,
Where they find happiness and fun.
Very few people look towards the moon,
Who changes itself soon....

But I'm different from everyone,
As I look towards both moon and sun....

Moon tells me that with time,
You can either grow yourself like mine,
And still be happy in hard time.....
But if you want to ignore all the cruelties and fear,
You can become small and disappear....

Sun tells me something different,
That we should never shy or bent,
Instead we should always be cheerful and bright,
And this will make our decisions positively right....
He also reminds me to help others,
To make everyone your friends and brothers.

One thing is said by both,
And to listen that I didn't at all loath,

"YOU ARE RESPONSIBLE FOR YOUR SURROUNDINGS
PROGRESS
SO NEVER MAKE SOMEONE DOWN OR DEPRESS."

So let me tell you,
What I learnt from these two,
That always be happy and cheerful,
And you should ignore to be fearful.....
When life goes expressionless,
Just keep smiling to this bloody mess,
Everything will be alright,
Next morning when sun shines bright.

Anjana Anilkumar

<u>LETHE</u>

Pain coursing through my veins,
Heart filled with nightmares,
Tired of sufferings which got no plans to end,
For,
You are still lingering in my mind.

Relentless search for a capsule or two,
Which will erase my memories
And ebb away my fears,
Ended up in the river,
The River Lethe.

River of forgetfulness, oblivion
And null memories
All I have to do is dip in the waters.

Happy, excited, ecstatic, I walk,
Finally I can be normal sans any pock,
Just one step away
From the spectacular Brooke

I am suddenly hit by what. Oblivion means.
Forgetting every moment

Unstrained as good or bad.

Yes, you are my painful memory.
But yes, you were the sweetest of them all.

I sit on the river bank,
Hit by this epiphany.
A train of thoughts
Running through.

It isn't oblivion that I want
Maybe a pinch of love
From somewhere else.
A pinch of understanding
That moving on isn't easy,
And finally a change of focus
From past nightmares to
New dreams.

Happy and content,
I leave the rocks.
I leave The Lethe
With no turning back.

Kashika Sachdeva

I sneak out of my house
Into the half awake world
Call out to my friends
We reach the sunrise point afterwards

It's a pretty morning, and sun rises above
Shines at us all, pouring it's warmth into our jackets
Which are half torn and shabby old?
But we sit there on the bench nonetheless
Quite accustomed to the rags, and the cold

I quickly make my way to Dadda's room
He tends to wake up early everyday!
But it's been a week since I saw him around
Oh! I've always been out and about in the day

I go back to my room, and change for work
Pick up my duffel bag, full of cigarettes and matches
Ready to begin a new day
Hoping to make a fortune after ages!

I bid momma good-bye, she looks at me and smiles like
everyday
But was there a tear building up in her eye?
I wasn't sure; she's always unreadable
Like today.

I jump out of the smallish gate,
Singing and whistling about,
Fresh dewdrops cover the plants on my way
Yellow tulips sway down the ditch; greenery all around

Cherishing the surreal beauty of the overhung clouds
I make my way to the mall road
It's usually empty this time, but not for me!
I have my customers ready- school children and the old!

I reach my usual place near the waterfall
As fallen leaves crunch beneath my feet
And I sell a packet or two to the old
And to children, with backpacks and potatoes sweet

As I hand over the matches, I witness an unusual sight
My sister comes running, wearing a dress all white
There are tear marks on her face
Evidence of a recent session of crying
And I can't help but ask, "What's the matter, Ruhi?"

But the words I hear, are the last ones I'd ever want to
again
"Dadda is dying, Preeti. You must come home."
The land subsided beneath me.
My knees wobbly and weak
The words didn't make no sense
How could this ever be?

But I mask my fear, for Ruhi was waiting
I ran back home, but my heart was aching
Dadda cannot die, he cannot, I know
What will momma say? Does she even know?

I stand near Dadda's room, and press my ears to the
door
There is a doctor, oh, and I can hear him talk
"You don't have any time left, the tobacco took your life,
I'm sorry sir, you must say good bye to your children
and wife
She has been crying since days, but I told you
Cancer is not a joke, it has spread a lot, too soon."

Cancer. Cancer. Cancer.

I fight back my tears, and force my legs inside
Dadda fidgets, and closes his eyes
"I love you Dadda, please don't go"
That is all. That is all I can mouth.

I rush back to my room, take out my duffel bag
Take it to the backyard, throw it down the hill
For it won't take no life now, the cigarette
And for a moment, I let my tears flow

And at a distance, I hear the cries
Ruhi. Momma.
Mourning voices, breaking bangles, cries; everyone
weeps
And I look up, into the vast morning sky "I will miss you,
Dadda", are the only words that come out of my mouth

Before the grief takes over, and I fall down.

Sakshi Shrivastav

I am a girl

Not your source of joy,

I am not a toy.

With which you can play,

And after this my feelings you can slay.

My feelings are like Dove,

Which want to fly in the sky of love.

I have sentiments,

I have emotions,

I won't allow you to hurt them for your lusty motions.

If I feel for you,

It is very pure and true

Don't give me a chance to hate you,

Otherwise my words will be very few,

But they will be as sharp as cold winter dew.

Accept me as I am,

If you can't,

Then stay happy with aunt.

I am not going to change,

I am not going to beg,

I don't care you smoke,

Or have a large peg.

At last,

Hate me if you can,

But trust me if I do,

I am a good heater then you.

So keep your attitude in your pocket,

Guys like you come in my life like fuel in rocket.

Swati Sudipta Barik

Dear A,

I think we're all breaking a little everyday like my brother's chipped front tooth. Little piece by piece. You, me, the girl that sits across me in biochemistry. How many months has it been? Seven. Everything is ending, slowly. Or should I say, beginning again? I don't like it.

The last time I heard your voice was on an angry Tuesday night. Rain stopped coming to my window and so did you. My mother keeps telling me that it's okay to leave and to be left behind. But I think that's only true in movies. What I feel is, anything but okay.

Absence is like presence with terms and conditions attached. You can't ask someone to be present without signing the consent form for absent. The days are galloping away from me on four legs. I keep looking for you in line breaks. In the gaps between two metaphors. But you're not hiding. Not anymore.

Some days I think about that day in the museum. Do you still have the photographs? My copies are covered in fingerprints. I bet yours are clean. It's okay. I don't blame you.

I remember reading Fitzgerald when the sky was a little bluer and you were here, one line stood out - there are all kinds of love in this world, but never the same love twice. I just hope the same is true for longing. [illegible]

[illegible]

Yours, [illegible]

S.[illegible]

[illegible]

Shubham Mudgil

<u>FALLEN</u>

I have fallen for your flaws,
Not for your dexterity but for innocence as a clause.
Never mercantile but for the common cause.
Fallen for that hesitation, that PAUSE.
HERE I stand as an apprentice,
Trying to break shackles to hold you close.
I stand at the brink of a new chapter,
Calling for you to widen the horizons,
Because baby, I want to be a sail to your BOAT,
Fragrance to your ROSE
And Power to your stature, your elegant POSE...

Adarsh Kumar Singh

The catastrophe

Driving on a cliff, steering my car left, straight deep
down the cliff.
Seeing, the catastrophe I created, or as others would
call this.
Just like when they saw me slowly walking on a road,
filled with fast moving cars.
It was the strange estrangement, which made it look all
so beautiful.

Just like when you saw that girl, cut the nerves of her
hand sinking so deep in that tub.

It only ever got us hurt, because I had the blade and I
chose to hold it where it was most edgy

Just like when they saw my pale face, thinking it was
time they let me go

Keep on asking, if they are okay?
Keep on guessing when the catastrophe takes place,
how did it happen ?
Fooling yourself , like you never knew

Deepanksha Wadhwa

Do you hear?

Do you hear the birds chirrup

At the break of dawn?
Have you heard the songs they sing
In the morning beyond the brawn?
Oh, haven't you ever felt
How they wake you up every day,
And sing to you beguiling melodies
And bring you liveliness and gay.

Do you hear the wind whoosh
Near your ear and tickling thee
Doesn't it make you laugh
And fill you with glee?

Do you hear the clouds rumble
Full of fury and rage?
And then cry to you 'pitter-patter'
And look down to you and daze?
Oh, haven't you ever felt
That they want you to soothe them,
Pacify their souls
And cure their scars and wem.

Do you hear the wolves howl
In the lone night,
And the cicadas click far away
While you sleep tight?
Oh, haven't you ever felt
That they tell you about their day,
They bicker all night
And go back to work when done with all they had to
say.

I hear them day and night
I hear the poetry they sing to me
I hear them at sundown and daylight
For I love their songs and melodies.

Samira Rahman

<u>Boketto Blues</u>

She gazed into the distant horizon,
A lone figure on the beach, overlooking
A black sea, waters swishing
Underneath her feet.

The sand under the hand is warm
From the day that ended,
Trying to hold in fist -
Like she tried to hold time, emotions and
Situations, a futile attempt.

A cigarette dangling in between
Her long fingers, ember-ish glow
Illuminating a little in the dark;
Doesn't touch her lips anymore

For she inhaled more
Than her share to consume it all.

All thoughts came to her, crowding
Her from all sides;
Clouding her vision, boketto
Into the velvety sky.

Aimless seems the life she desired,
Pointless in living anymore;
Crucified to a living that is painful,
Battling the war within and outside
With her soul.

Scars adorn the soul and tattered pieces
She dearly holds;
Where would she go now?
How long could she hold?
The water soothes and touches
Like a blue lover, and she smiled absently
But consoling whom?

Riya Adlakha

Hope to have a daughter !

I hope to someday have a daughter,
A daughter of my own,
A daughter as a niece,
Or a daughter I adopt,
Who will be bold as a lioness,
No less than an angel.
She will trend in my dreams,
Which will be filled with creams?
She will be a pure heart ,
Dealing with the impure ones .
Her pure smile and innocent eyes
Would never by devastate by those brutal hypocrites.
I will know all her heart's desires
And keep fulfilling them by fighting all fires.

She will be an ultimate paradox,
The irony,
The valorous,
The enough !

Jayeesh Arora

<u>THE UNSEEN SIDE</u>

Tell me what do you see?
Do you see another side to the darkness,
Or is it just me wishing for someone to hold onto,
I came here with a soul as pure and bright as glass.

But like glass it may shatter
Like glass it may get scratched
And like glass it may lose its shine.

For now, I walk the path all alone
That I too am not fond of,
A lie is what I am living,

Grief is a friend
And what I dream of can't be reached
Then what is happiness?

I want to find out,
I want to see what lies beyond this life full of pain,
I am alone I know,
But it would be nice to see someone walk beside me,
'I want' is one thing I need to get rid off,
'I need' is another thing that will ruin me,
'Me' does it really matter.

Navika Kaith

<u>Reverie</u>

The little Nightingale, she sang.
With abandon absolute, and
Effortless harmonization.
She strained into the distance
Of the still, silent night;
That welcomed her rhythm
Into its fond embrace,
And swayed in complement
To her gentle trill.

But what did she sing about,

You ask?
The little bird sang of love,
Of young, willful, romantic love.
All that dreams are made up of.
Her notes had stemmed,
From the fantastical confines
Of amorous verse and tales of bliss,
That blossomed her fancy into
Her voice. And yet,
When she sang, she never reached
Her crescendo.
An answer lost in the break
Before her highest note.

But why was it so,
You ask?
Because the little bird sang from desire,
Imaginary, whimsical, enchanting desire.
Of furtive glances and lovelorn sighs,
And vignettes rolling,
Before her eyes.
For the lulling melody of her hum,
Had branched from inexperience.
The mingling breaths and
Clashing skins was all,
Her imagination.

And time left there was still
For her yearning to acquire
Intensity in emotion,
Before she reached her echoing climax,
And all her innocence was lost.

Thus the little Nightingale, she sang.
In wistful, longing, aspiring notes,

She sang.

Pratistha Kharbanda

You treated me
Like a muse
For one of your essays
On Renaissance
But I'm just shards
Of broken glass
Be careful
Not to touch me
I'll bleed you dry
Until you can't cry anymore
My lovers before you
Said I reminded them of

Plath's 'Paralytic'
And now all I can think of
Is blasting my head off
In a microwave
You said I tasted like
Despair
Right before you left
Me without a kiss
And I swear
I could feel the aftertaste
On my tongue
But your hands
Reeked of heartache
When you tucked my hair
Behind my ear
And after you left
I cut them off
And dyed them blue
So it wouldn't just
Be a feeling
Now all my wounds
Look like
You in a vintage photograph
From the 1860s
So don't tell me
Those ghosts don't exist
When all I can bring myself to think about
Is how sometimes,
Graveyards
Can make
The most beautiful
Of homes.

Dev Chopra

<u>PRISM</u>

I am a human
My life is free
Each passing day
More branches on the tree

Must remember everything
I may just write it down
Alas If I forget something

Do I lose my crown?

Roles and definitions
Ought to fulfill them all
Fail one or a few
The blocks are going to fall

I have friends
And so do they
Failed to have their back
Can I still ask them to stay?

I claim to love her
And so does she
Near comes a day
Where I need you
And you need me

Or If I may
We need we

Simultaneously
Does it make sense ?
Well I claimed to love her
And so did she

Being a child
Should I always lie?
How does this work
If it still makes them cry

Learning new things
Not once should I stop
Where is the switch
For this machine in the top

My health and education
I must keep track
My dreams like books
In the dusty old rack

But No,
I shall follow them fine
Weighing expectations
Do I not count mine?

Only if you could
See me as a whole
Even the strong stick breaks
When you take it out alone

Along all this
I must have fun
Hope you don't mind
I if I drink that rum?

If only it were that easy
Playing such a gamble on health
Aren't there plenty other ways
But is this how I lose my wealth?

-DC

Yashashree Raghuwanshi

Filled with emotions, I write my heart out,
Not fearing about the pages nor the people in my
whereabouts.

I cradle a cloud inside me,
Heavy and hazy.
Down I shatter in million pieces,
It's dark, you cannot see.
You ponder and wander around for just a while,

Standing near a street light, grinning like a juvenile.
You are drenched and soaked, but now you see me,
Fragmented in million silver threads;
Filling a puddle to its brim.

Your heart.

Filled with imagination, I paint my vividness,
About the scent full sunrises in the embrace of wild
wilderness.

I paint my sky all indigo and violets,
Dabbing my brushes dry in your shirt before I forget.
But soaked and drenched you are,
The blot dissipates like the dawn rays;
Not much to despair, yet so far.
I swirl my tiny bristle in the darkness of the night before,
Carefully intricating small seagulls offshore.
You give a voice to my barren horizon,
I respond to your cold fingers with utmost passion.

Maanushi Sodhi

Fragments of the glass that fell;
Fell, that cleaved up the heart.
Fragments pitching the bickers of the shatters
On the floor;
Perforate me, through the flesh of my jaw line.

Fragments of the castle we built;
Built, on the feeble and effete foundations.

Fragments of the unwavered sinew
And of the bricks crushed to grains;
Hit now like the sparks from a metal sheet proletarian.

Fragments of the organism banking upon the host,
Host, whose movements surmise either a mimeo twin
Or death.
Fragments of the succumbed cocoon,
How, Horrors the drop in the boiling water.

Fragments- the little pieces, we collected;
Collected in our hands and on laps,
Those that lapsed.
Fragments schismed, ruptured the both;
Pierced underneath my feet all the more.

FRAGMENT. (Noun) a small part broken off or separated
from something.

It's anything but small. .

Fragments of me,
Fragments of you,
Fragmented us.

Anant Seth

It rained today. I'm pretty sure it's not supposed to in
November,
But that's how arbitrary things are, I guess.
Do you remember how I used to bug you with this
information though: that I just love the rains,

The fresh dusty aroma of the first shower, the clarity of
air,
The majestic growling of the clouds?
I will never cease to think of that one time we slow
danced in the rain,
When you had my headphones on.
I couldn't even hear the song that was playing but I
guess what you're listening to was supernumerary for
both of us in that moment.
I could literally feel happiness radiate from your smile,
not more than an inch away from my face.
I hadn't felt anything so real and overwhelming since
forever. However, as I looked at the person your eyes
were reflecting, he wasn't nearly as happy as you were.
The sound of thunder sunk me into a cavernous
introspection of what I felt for you, and it was then I
realized,
You were at the right place, at the right time,
But with the wrong person.
"Grey or blue?" You asked.
I didn't have an answer.
That was the last rain we ever shared, the last time we
ever danced,
And the last time we ever saw each other.
I read somewhere that we only accept the love we think
we deserve,
So we drifted apart for one of us deserved better.
Just one of us.
I'm sitting here on the balcony of my apartment
watching the leftovers of this unexpected rain to
evaporate into nothing,
When it hits me.
I hate the rains. I lied to you about it when we first met,
And had been constantly lying to myself ever since.

Though there's one thing about the rains that soothes
me.
It's grey and blue.

Sukeerat Kaur Channi

Give me love
All kinds of love

Give me poetry too
Each tarnished word
Blurry photos
Hugs
Light kisses
And forgotten leaves of the autumn
I'll be ok then
I think
I won't be so broken then
I think

Light is for another hour
Teach me to stay calm
As I listen to my dark
Every shameful whisper
Teach me
The lilt of the rain soaked puddles
All the weight of all that life
The sheer momentum
Of how to be
Teach me
I'll be ok then
I think
I won't be so lonely then
I think

Tell me your dreams
Not your dreams dreams
Your little dreams
The color you imagine
Every time you look at me
The French windows of your heart
That opens into poetry
Tell me
Your ugly that's too beautiful

For the world
Your mutilated
Your silly
Your soft
Tell me
Then we'll be silent together
I think
Kind of ok together I think

Nitin Mukesh

It was dark everywhere,

And it was raining,
The water on the road,
Slowly draining.
Soon rain became heavy,
And weather was cold,
Sitting beside the window,
It was a scene to behold.
But there was a movement,
On the road I have seen.
I got close to window,
But it felt like a dream.
Someone was going,
It was night so late,
In the profound rain,
He was wet.
Suddenly thunder shown,
And I saw some food in hand.
Probably he was a worker,
And his age was grand.
It's all destinies,
Some sleep few works,
Life is balanced for some,
For few it hurts..

Manu Chauhan

<u>THE SCAR FACED WARRIOR</u>

Countless battles of frozen pain,
Scar marked his battle torned face,

Clots of blood flooded his veins,
Wounds covered his blood bathed frame,
He watched the roots burn down,
He watched new reign began,
His unending life was a boon,
The horrible curse of immortality,
He watched with his naked eyes,
The rivers red with martyrs cries,
He walked through the paths of doom,
Snatching himself from the sands bygone,
Stood there with thumping heart,
Heart beating a frivolous task,
Dashing past the curtains of time,
He stood there with tears drying,
He stood there with tears drying.....

- M

Rachita Oberoi

I waft words upon white paper
As she sways me to her thoughts
Of her love and of her loss.

My ink flows like kohl onto the sheets
As if making love, drip by drip
Painting her black monsoon
And her sunken ship.
She held me that lonesome night
Yearning for her lover's touch
Her fingers swirled around me tight
And her grip feels like my lover's touch.
So I tell her that he cares, not for her, but the number of
his affairs.
Tears roll down her cheeks
For all she knows he's between the sheets
And thinks about it a bit too much that
He's embracing one of his lover's touch.
So I tell her don't you care
It was nothing more than a nightmare.
She pressed me against the paper to say
The sun didn't shine again today
But life can be just as beautiful much
If you let the moonlight be your lover's touch

Kash Sheokand

My parents don't sleep in the same bed.
To a six year old girl,
That never mattered.
But to a seven year old girl, it does.
She knows that other kids

Have parents who sleep together,
In the same bed,
Every night.
To a seven year old girl,
It doesn't matter that her parents
Don't talk about stuff.
But an eight year old girl knows.
Other parents have conversations,
Small ones, big ones.
An eight year old girl doesn't know
What an arranged marriage is.
But a nine year old does.
What a nine year old doesn't know
Is that her parents fight.
But a ten year old girl knows
That her mother thinks her father isn't enough
And her father can't stand her mother.
Fortunately, a ten year old girl
Doesn't know
About divorces.
But an eleven year old girl does.
She also knows that the only reason
Her parents are still married
Is because they can't get rid of her.
A twelve year old knows
That she's a burden
A constant reminder
Of two lives gone astray.
A fifteen year old young woman knows
That whatever her life brings her
A sad broken marriage shouldn't be included.
A sixteen years old girl knows better
Than to call her friends over for a night out.
What if they find
That her parents are messed up?

An eighteen year old girl knows
That she wasn't the product of love
But of a tradition.
Of hate.
Of unsaid things.
Ripped stitches.
Lifeless birthdays.
An eighteen year old looks at every other five year old
girl
And wishes she never finds out.

SCAS

I was 18,
I remember.
Going from my college to home,

The day I was dismembered.

Someone groped my breast in the transport,
And before I knew, it was gone.
I thought it was a mistake,
But I didn't know the journey was going to be long.

One after another it happened,
I was too scared to raise my voice.
And before I knew,
It wasn't even my choice.

Because what do I know about my body?

I was pushed aside in the empty bus,
With six men over me.
Ripping off my clothes open,
Opening my body for them to see.

I was pinned down on the floor,
Trying to scream as loudly as I could.
Only falling on deaf ears,
Hearing, "Fuck her as a man should".

"You're a slut, meant to be used by us",
"Deep inside you, we shall drill"
"We are the superior gender",
"You don't have any will".

Because what do I know about my body?
I woke up two weeks later,
In a hospital with white walls.
With my family trying to fight the society,
Which said that I was false.

"Why didn't she dress up modestly?",
"Why didn't she call them brother?".
"Why was she out so late at night?",
"All of it led to her being smothered".

For the first time,
I felt bad about being a woman.
And the way everyone was speaking,
I wondered if I was even human.

Because what do I know about my body?

Then the doctor told me,
I was pregnant with a child.
My tears were out of my eyes,
And my thoughts stopped to flow.

The rapist would have parental rights,
Over this child, I got but never wanted.
That is the justice I got for my sufferings,
And my life was unremarkably haunted.

My future came crashing down,
I couldn't even abort for my dreams.
My life was ruined,
Maybe, I was meant to live this way it seems.

Because what do I know about my body? Men do.

-S

Shivanshi Bhadhouria

<u>Summer evening</u>

Sipping on iced tea,
Reading Riding Hood,
With scraped knees,
Covered with band aids,
I found love
Kept in pockets
With little holes,
In a jacket that was too
Warm for the weather.

So while I read Picasso
And used acid
To paint,
I found my muse
Hidden somewhere
In the memories
Of a past life,

So I wove poems
On magic,
Sprinkled ash
On paper,
Mixed colors
On floorboards
Made tea
In a coffee pot.

And I used up
The rest of that summer evening
To bind pages

Written on sorcery,
In red ink,
With hair strands
That Rapunzel left behind.

~

Sb

Archana Gajbinker

<u>Rain</u>

Every time you drop your soul on ground,
Swinging in the air with a pleasant sound,
The best thing in you I have found ,
Is the happiness you spread around ,

The way grass blush with a silent Melody ,
When your drops touch their delicate body .

The way you nurture this beautiful earth ,
With every drop , you shower faith .

The way those mountains relax calmly ,
When your water flows through their valley .

The way humans find their lost happiness ,
When your each drop fills their emptiness .

Surprised by the way you spread this affection
I looked at the sky and asked a question ,
" How are you filled with so much of celebration,? ,
Did you ever fell tired of your situation ?"

Looking at me sky grinned and replied
" I hold more drops of tears than you do ,
But I choose a right time to fall through ,
I make my tears worth enough to gift you ,
I never make my sorrow win over my view ."

Listening to the beautiful story of sky and rain,
I understood that spending those nights in vain ,

Is not the solution for our pain .
Getting over it will help us live again ,
Letting everything out will help us survive again .
Becoming more kind with every pain we sustain ,
Spreading happiness will be the ultimate gain .

Aayushi Verma

When your feelings are numb,
And heart is cold
When you feel like you're drowning,
In the ocean of your mistakes;
The evil seems never to halt,
Like the perpetual darkness which you see deep below
I want you to struggle through the pain,
Fight for your breathe.
And when you're out in the open sand,
I'll call you a fighter,
'Cause you made it through what seemed impossible
I'll call you a warrior,
'Cause you almost killed a party of yourself when you
were low
And when you'll look back at it
Tears might roll down, but of the victory that you own.

Deepanshi Rao

You said you liked my hair

Open and loved me when I smile

You embraced me when in tears

And held on for a long while

They say it's really tough

Tough to let your loved ones go

But people change like seasons

The warmest hearts turn cold too

To the boy who over loved me

And couldn't stay for long

I truly deserve someone better

Who holds on even if it's wrong

You too deserve better

Cause we clearly weren't meant to be

The truth was right in front of us

But we were too much in love to see.

Isha Adhikari

<u>Dusky</u>

"She is a little dusky but when she applies make-up you won't see the difference." Her mother's shrill voice ricocheted through her eardrums echoing in her brain.

That day, her soft voice didn't soothe her legs that ached or calmed her ever-so jittery nerves, rather it was the cause of which something broke.

When a glass shatters,
It makes some noise but what when a heart breaks?
When a heart breaks, there's a funeral.
No, heaven doesn't cry, it's silent like prayer time, to a god who'd rest her soul for another of his child now turned cold.

Dusks always had been more beautiful than the dawn for her.
The serene sky, the chilled night brought her peace; a time to reflect on her entire day, to reach out to her soul's depth.

She would wonder if liking the end made her evil? But, then she never really understood when her art teacher would tell her to mix crimson, yellow and scarlet for a sunny sky.

She liked the night because it was simple, just paint the white canvas black. And, when her spine chilled, her eyes yearned for light, she'd add some stars and make it a starry sight.

The books she read always said that black was the purest of all, but, was there mockery hidden in between those lines?

Maybe, when she skimmed through the pages, her glasses might have turned foggy or she might have mixed up another line. She is messy, you see, what can you expect from a girl so dusky?

She always wondered why white hair was bad but white skin good? Maybe there is an epic after all for such rules.

That certain day, she thought of that comment as a compliment, she fraternized with cosmetic the other night.

It was summer, you see, when she washed her face, the foundation peeled off, leaving a canvas a few shades lighter than charcoal black.

Few years later, now, she is all grown-up and packed with degrees, she is the face of her own company with not a single drop makeup matching her real beauty; her brain.

Renita D'souza

They say
Love is either
As fiery as wildfire
Or as cold as ice
And that you will either burn to the ground
Or be stuck to it, frozen to death
Arms open wide
Forever cemented in the middle of an unheard plea

But I like
To be rooted
In all the in-betweens of it-

The way
You learnt sign language
Back in college
Just so you would be
The only boy
Who could talk to me

The way you kiss my nose in the morning
Before leaving for work
And the way you walk out the door, and run right back
If you ever forget
To go through with your precious morning routine.

The way we fight-
All soft punches and mouthed curses and silent screams
Till you grip my arms
And pull me in
And plant one of your signature wet kisses on my
forehead
And sign

"You're an idiot".
The way I can't keep my hands off of your naked chest
And the way I lay my head down on it
And fall asleep
To the quiet thuds
Of your irregular heartbeat.

The way you switch on loud rock music
And we slow dance to the feel of the beats on the
speaker
At 1 am
Under stars
That seems to twinkle brighter
Whenever you're around.

The way
You like your tea
With exactly two sugars
But you never complain
When I forget
To add one.

The way
You bring me food
On days when I can't get up off the couch
And sit silently by my side
Even though
The last thing I want to do
Is be around people
And the way
I always put aside my favorite book
To watch your stories unfold instead.

The way
You swing dance

With my inner demons
To a song I will never hear-
A melody that makes you seem forlorn
And the way
You smile
Right after I escape
The monsters under my bed
To run straight into your arms.

The way we never talk about love
Or how we had our hearts broken
Before we ran into each other
And the way your warm lips
Feel on mine
And how your cold fingers
Trace sentences on my spine.

The way
You sign every morning
"I like our temperature"
And then shoot me one of your cheeky grins
Because darling
We both know
We refuse to go so far
As to be burnt alive
Nor attempt to go nowhere
And end up freezing to death
But damn it all
If this in-between land
Doesn't feel like fucking paradise.

Adhya manocha

<u>WHAT DOES LOVE LOOK LIKE?</u>

1. When they make tea for you waking up early in the morning, though their eyes are worn out because of everyday fights and the scars you gift them along with it. Also, they never forget to add those 2 extra spoons of sugar and a tinge of ginger just the way you like it.

2. When they wait for you to come back home with their eyes worn out but hopes too high. But maybe, they have forgotten that you will only love them by saying words which will hit them like a sword piercing their heart, the same way noise cuts silence.

3. When they feel like an accomplishment when you praise them. Maybe they have forgotten that you are not the first raindrop touching the droughty land, but just a wine bottle which is only meant for intoxicating people.

4. When they still try to keep the sunflowers of this love alive by watering them every day. Maybe they have forgotten that its winter and the weeds have already grown in the garden.

5. When they want to run back to the place from where they came but are afraid to leave the darkness behind. So, they take candles in both hands and again start consuming them to light you up. Maybe they have forgotten that you have become darkness, so dark that even your shadows have left you. But they are still here, burning them slowly and silently, though this silence

echoes so loudly that it feels like a thunder light that rips them apart.

6. When they just want to run and take one of the blades out from the bed drawer for the 100th time and think of slitting their wrist and freeing themselves from your darkness. But they STOP. They stop because your thought scares them. They fear that there would still be someone who would shed tears for them after they will be gone, and they cannot see your eyes getting wet.

But maybe they are wrong. It is not you who loves them but they who love you and live for you, though it makes them feel dead now.

After all, nobody can come back from a coffin after getting buried in it. But for the very first time, somebody's coffin is responsible for their death.

You are the coffin and they are slowly becoming a carcass.

Aastha takkar

Today I met a happy soul , accompanied by a flurry of
thoughts!
I could see a violent desire hiding in her inferno eyes.
I could see the beauty hidden in her fragile vibes.
Yes, she was a girl of seven , selling flowers at the signal
which was her own heaven.
And ,I kept staring at 'her' world!
She then approached me to buy those odorous things
,saying HAPPY VALENTINE'S!
And my heart skipped a beat at that time .
How could I feel more torment in my heart ,when I saw
that happily ever after in her smile ?
And I bought the whole bunch, because we make our
own beauty and mend our own pain before we half-love
this world we disdain.

Parul Karn

All I am learning is love…
More and more of it…
Even if I don't have you
I have come very far.
I'm learning love more than before
Even if I won't see you again
Even if I won't tease you for silly things anymore
The sound of your voice will still be musical in my mind
I'm learning more music than before
Through your silence
Even when you're gone
You're the "ocean" by the "native"
Be it that way
Like the little fairy lights we saw together
I don't know if you paid attention to it
You have no idea how it soothes my soul
Our crazy stories so similar yet so poles apart
You make me believe that every crazy thing is possible
So my once in a lifetime
Thanks to you…

Anirudh Puranik

I told her again.
I told her again..
I told her again that what I thought was gone, actually
never left
My ship never left
The coast it clung to
I told her that I was always on the same shore,
The difference being -I was dying to tell you what I feel
the first time I realized it,
But this time I was dying to ensure that you don't catch a
hint of the depth.
I told her that despite all this, just her presence was
enough to get me through the stormy sea
I told her that inspite of trying a number of times,
I was not able to get over the waves
I told her that I was waiting for the ferry to arrive,
despite knowing that it wouldn't

Somewhere down the line,
I felt I was never a part of her story
But even this did not stop me from loving her,
To stop and think the wrong I was doing to myself,
To stop myself from investing in a bank where I knew , I
would be robbed every day,
To stop being a companion to the one who would never
sail with me,

To stop getting closer and closer
Again and again, closer
and spend rest of my days in a miserable state trying to
figure out ,how to start from scratch again.
How to stay afloat, again
To stop falling for the same person again and again.
To stop- just thinking about all the unsuccessful stops
and do something about it

We started having sessions, after every few months,
weeks, even days when it felt like my ship was about to
sink
Where I would tell her all of this again and again,
Of what I felt
Of what I feel
Of what I tried
And what I incurred from this 100th unsuccessful
attempt was that with every such session,
I would get the strength to tackle this uncontrollable
feeling
Hitting me wave upon wave
for some time,
Not that I started craving for these sessions but to be
honest I did look up to such things and saw it sometimes
before hand
But I never asked her what she felt after any of these,
My Ship was rarely concerned about the anchor that
kept me ashore.

Probably because this was the only thing that gave me
relief that I just couldn't afford to keep her as my priority
even in the last resort that gave me peace.
After these sessions ,I felt like I could end life at this
positive note,
I felt I could fight off all storms and sail all seas.

She was actually that contingent plan for which I had no
plan B ready,
Coming out of nowhere like a wind of spontaneity!
Even in a war, eventually somebody has to lose
Life is tough and so are most of the things that we really
want in life,
And I am fortunate that this time I am the one who loses
you,
because in order to sail,
My ship must leave behind the anchor that was you.

Sambhav Chalana

Of all the eternally sleepless nights by the door,
For you keep ringing my doorbell to visit the neighbors.
I always know it's you yet I open the door
With both our drinks in my hand, hoping
Hoping that maybe this time you'll come in and we drink
through the night.
But as I sat on the usual night sipping on both our
glasses,
I thought about your letters and
How you complained I never wrote one,
Your letters with, to and by my first name,
Your letters where you only wrote about the grand
fancies of nature and how you saw me in them,
Your letters which I no more read.

For, love, I don't belong at any of those exhibitions of
nature that you left me.

Beaming at the night sky,
You always landed me on the moon with its beauty
"Eternal", you said, "Despite its scars".
O how I wish I were the moon and not the shooting star
How I wish shooting stars could wish upon themselves.

Walking by the sea,
Hand in hand,
Near the lamp post where you left me.
The same lamp post which fell for the waters so bad,
It lost all its radiance just to make the sea look beautiful
under its light.
I hoped, as you walked away,
That you'd feel me in your hands that we held and
return.

I hoped that you realized it wasn't under the light but
the hands where I belonged.
I have a picture of you from under that crazy "lover", as
they say, of the sea, as you were walking away;
The last picture I have of you.

Here is a letter with, to and by my first name
To your address, which might drop you at my exact
address
In the hope that you pick me up from all these places
and we take a walk home,
For the due drink?

To, my love
With Love,
Love.

Gaurav Chaudary

<u>You? Are You?</u>

Is it me, or just an effort to be myself of what I did never want to become. Our lives are full of oxymorons. It's sometimes a minute that runs years and years in our heads or sometimes it's a long day, of which, not even a minute passes worth living. What takes it all, is an effort to find ourselves, who we really are? Life waits to find a life, yet things are left unanswered throughout. What these answers are for? Isn't just a life living to find these puzzles solved out, life? Isn't life this only? Our powerful souls seek earth, so when it falls, it hits hard.
We eventually wait, everybody does, everyone has to.
Wait till when? Till life.
Wait for what? For life.
The unfaithful time is what assures to define meanings, creating even jumbled emotions to ask for more answers to life. Oxymoronic life is!
What makes you feel good, makes you lustrous to have it. If it isn't here, you feel bad and other things don't please anymore.
Emotions are not material, yet material reflects them all. What emotions are? Are they what you choose to, want to, feel. Or they make you want and choose things for yourself. Do you really choose to become what you want to? That's a parody.
What is life without people? Is it worth living? Or it provides a race to live? A place to explore yourselves in context of others?
Is it you? -About your life?
Or is it about everyone with whom your life is affected with? Nothing assures Nothing.
Eventually you wait, till life! Till you! Till end.
You just have to!
~ Ar.

Tejashree Murugan

Looking down from the airplane window
I see a painting
With swirls of color like a Van Gogh
Yellow sunlight streaming through hazy clouds
People make up those tiny specks, amongst other things
It's funny how my entire happiness revolves around one
of those miniscule dots
Because you are one of those dots
But when I'm near you, it's different
The air between us crackles with electricity
I'm aware of every little thing
How our shoulders bump together
How your crooked little smile resembles a comma
How your eyes sparkle when you think I'm not watching
But I am
And when you notice my gaze, and blush, and look
down
I have to fight off the compulsion to look at your feet too
And to see whether they're as perfect as the rest of you

Phalguni Jagadeesh

<u>Love hate life</u>

Not all the time,
Love ends with happiness.
Not all the time,
Love gives peace.
Not all the time,
Love has joy.
It's filled with
Mixed emotions and balanced life.

There's hatred and sorrows,
There are scars and bruises.
Love and hate are interlinked
And that's where everything connects.

Trust, hope, understanding and belief,
Four pillars of four letters (LOVE).
Break one or make one,
It's in the way you take it.

But, where there's hate, there's love,
Where there's love, there are emotions,
Where there are emotions, there's life
And where there's life, there's happiness.

Shivangi Pahwa

<u>Under The Same Sky-</u>

I have always hated romantic clichés.
I've seen people say
"Atleast we're under the same sky"
when they talk about long lost love,
with a sigh.
I'm sure so have you
so tell me this,
is this the reality
you want to live in?
Because it's not just your supposed love
that lives under the same sky.
There are rapists that live here.
There are murderers that do.
We live under the same sky, too.
Stop using a phrase
that comforts your conscience
with profound lies
that bring no actual solace in your life.
We all live under the same sky
because we're all humans
born on the earth
that didn't bother with different skies,
Only different times.
So let's face reality in this one.
We all make mistakes,
And we all blame each other.
We practice violence,
Yet scream for non-violence.

We're all not fine
But say that we are.
We're all stupid.
We're all fake.
Yet we all have kindness inside us.
It is our actions that separate us,
And not our location.
And do you know why?
Because we all live under the same sky.

Pooja Trivedi Raval

Like all other people in the world
I never find the satisfactory word.

Finding the reason why I am here
Is always my mind wants me to ear

I always have the one fear
Can anyone trust or like to hear?

I get to know that I can teach
Very effectively the subjects each

It might be my purpose to have life
Or else it would be found and led by the life.

Dhiren Gor

Can I tell you something?
I like in my life the one thing

I don't like dance
Nor like to take a chance..

I don't like to sing
For the music in my life to bring

I don't like to hurt anyone
Ibaleays try to help someone..

It might be the purpose to be alive
With humanity for others to survive

Himani Raval

Why should I need to worry about future
It's all have been decided with my born for future;

My likings my choices and my nurture in childhood
It's the message of universe to be good

Unknowingly I am doing the things
Which are perfect and going to give me wings

I am less bothered with the plan
And still having the perfection in glance

Thank you universe to plan for me
To provide the best decision maker for me..

Manvi Sharma

<u>Fantasizing Reel</u>

Deciding upon my fate
I cursed those fantasies,
The fantasies
That had been the fairytales to many.
Since I was naïve,
Glittering all my imaginations
I made the mistake
Of, bringing those pages to the life of uncertainty.
Believing in the morals of closed books,
Loving makes me go high,
When I read those lines of vain
In the name of rationality.
I burnt those pages,
Reality turned down to ashes
All I was left with the smoke
And the white lies of reality.
Shattering dreams,
And broken promises
I searched for those legends
Who didn't have any solution to this obscenity.
Now, that I am lost
In the red ink of love,
I do not find a pen
To write the lines of purity.

Oh Lord! Save me from this deceptive world,
I am not the one who belongs here
Make me that girl,
Who is always looked upon every time I read.

Harsh Bhardwaj

"Darkness is what remains"
I wrote.
Dreams are
Boats, battered with age,
We ride upon
Hoping
To cross this river
Of blood
In which shines
The stars, which have been
Long dead!

Time doesn't justify their death,
Nor our life, it does.
It eradicates everything
And ultimately itself!

It's a shore
(Where silence is yet
Intact)
I reach with closed eyes.
My father lost himself somewhere here,
They say,
That night

When he came to throw his gun.
But that was years ago.
Now
Is a woman
Who often visits me
In my poems.
She stands
On the shore opposite
And throws her lamp into the river
"Darkness is what remains
Between you and me; "
She yells
"It's something that bridges us! "
And
I put my flute
On fire
To prove her wrong.
And it's not tears
But my melody
That runs on my cheek.

"Time is a graveyard"
I have opened my eyes
And wrote.
Stars die a harsh death,
I always knew;
They become Iron in their death.
And we?

I wrote "home"
And put blade to my veins.
I have lost myself slowly
Over the years
While writing poems
And ultimately

"Love"
Was what I wrote
And jumped out of the window!

Syeda Tahira Abidi

<u>FLAMES</u>

Burning amidst the flames
The scars I carved on my canvas,
Are incessantly yelling their fate
And yet I charge on them tremendous.

Fear of being tormented or scattered
Has never inflected my intent
To be a potter's craft
And shape my mud by draft
.
In the magisterial furnace,
Glowing with fire and vehemence.
Where it's blinding radiance and insensate impel
assured
Solace to a flickering soul,
For the pain it had inflicted.
To smelt my metal and to celebrate the making of a
sword.

Bhavya M Jain S

<u>My Ethics Of Life</u>

ETHICS ARE MUST IN THY LIFE

Thank God daily & bow down for everything.
Pray each day for unasked gifts & strength.
Learning must never stop.
Be down to earth.
Value time.
Never under estimate anyone.
Respect everyone.
Be simple, humble, polite, passionate.
Give self time.
Love unconditionally,
See others inner beauty..!!
Try, giving up is not an option.
Success has no ends.
Humanity matters.
Make life colorful.
Spread happiness....

ETHICS MAKE US WHO WE WANT TO BE. VALUE THEM, FOLOW THEM, THEY WILL LEAD YOU...

These are a few ethics of my life,
Have you discovered yours?

Rashi Soni

Taher. Taher believes in God.
"He's one lucky man you see Taasha?"
I look at him all puzzled up.
"He gets to look at all of us"
The most vulnerable, honest shape of us.
I look up at the receding pinks in the sky and suddenly
feel naked.
Thoughtful. Disturbing rather.
Taher was the most romantic man I knew.
He could even romanticize the dust jammed up in his
attic.
So graceful. Almost effortless.
So much that it's scary.
Scary cold.
But beautiful.
Like those cold fragrant winds that arrive shortly before
the winter.
Sending shivers down my spine.

Too hot.
He reminds me of "ostyt"- a cup of tea left on the table,
too hot.
But after you walk to the next room and return, too cold.
So cold that it's scary.
"Mamori tai"
I will always protect you.
What he does not understand is that people are nothing
but unforgettable bones of dust.
But Taher was the most romantic man I knew.
He could even romanticize dust.

Nil Dey

<u>Poem</u>

Long was that lonely time
Wondered I for the first time in my life
Why is it so that I have no one to rhyme

But are at all my thoughts real

Then suddenly I remember

Why did I stop reading
Why did I stop writing
Why did I stop following my passion
It was some to which thing I got never bored
Rest all was for just a limited session

Yes I was running around fake looks
Too late did I understand
That my real friends are my books

Yes I was all behind the straps of the real
Due to which I was losing all that zeal

May be too late
But at least I understood my real fate..

© Nil, " The introvert with 14 inch biceps"

Chhavi Bambha

There are days I choose conflict,
Put myself in fights that don't matter,
Battles so insignificant they shouldn't be picked,
Sometimes all there is just chatter.

When you focus on a black dot, that's all you see.
Same the chaos, that's all I feel.
Somehow, that's what helps me escape because the
bigger questions, I can't shake.

I win narrow quests; forget serious battles
I cross the finish line, but never win.

Chetna Yadav

<u>SALT</u>

It was the summer morning in 2000
When I first met her
She wasn't smiling but she was happy
but soon it just went warer
It was jealousy
She thought she had lost all her embassy
But soon she came to realize
It was me she could penalize
Days passed
"Where did the time flew?" I asked

From saying "it's all your fault"
To her being as important as a pinch of salt
From watching Tom and Jerry
To fighting over a piece of cherry
I remember when people asked me if she was my sister
And I used to say "wrong! Cousin Mister"
She was not my blood
But she did save me from each tear flood
For the sake of all few of those hugs
I am going to tell you what really bugs
The day has arrived and she has to go away
Oh boy don't I just wish she could stay
I still want to wear those similar frocks
And continue all those unfinished talks
There were punches and kicks
Isn't it weird how the clock always ticks
She was never a flawless dove
But she did give me unconditional love
Without her I don't know what I'll be
For if I am salt then she is my sea

Rahul Jena

I met someone who has changed my life in a better way.
She lifted me up when I was going through the most
tough time..
She has always motivated me not by the sugar coated
words but by her actions, her style was different.
For me she was the person who has helped me to find
the real me.
When I was lost in the crowd and then from somewhere
a hand came along and pulled me out of the crowd.

Those hands created a strong grip.
Those hands helped me to find my goals.
Those hands promised me that they won't leave.
Those hands taught me to stand out of the crowd
without shaking.
And then one day when I entered into the crowd again ,
I didn't feel like being lost instead of it I felt motivated
and powerful and this miracle happened just because of
those hands.
But where she is now?
I lost her hand in the same crowd where I had held her
for the first time.
And I am lost again.
Oh hand please come back.

- Rahul

Shreya Arora

<u>An ode to the moon</u>

The light on an endlessly dark night;
A symbol of god for some;
A cure to so many writers' blocks;
Comfort when the world seems like chaos;
The definition of love for some;
And a ray of hope for many;

Sometimes, the only healer of a broken heart.

Maybe like humans, you have phases too; Is it because
you get tired too;
Tired of spreading your light even when you're
surrounded by darkness yourself;
Tired of being so much to everyone;
Tired of never being appreciated for all that you do?

I always wonder, what makes you come back again and
again. But I hope you know how much you mean, when
you're ready to burn yourself out again.

92

The 52 Poets

Srishti Nautiyal

My thoughts needed a way out and I find my solace in writing
Insta : Srishti97

Vanshika Aggrawal

My name is Vanshika Aggarwal.
I live in Gurugram, Haryana.
I have completed my schooling from D.A.V. Public School,
Sec-14, Gurugram.
Contact: 1normallamron1@gmail.com
Insta : abnormalgarl

Anjana Anilkumar

Anjana Anilkumar, a 21 year old girl from Kerala, recently graduated in Economics Hons. from Sri Venkateswara College. Loved to be known in her pen name, Iris. Active in insta @iris_zephyros. That's where you can find me.

Kashika Sachdeva

I'm Kashika Sachdeva, pursuing an honours in course of Psychology from University of Delhi. And no, I cant read minds. When I am not dancing or writing, you can find me singing my heart out or indulging in introversion while casually reading a novel.

Sakshi Shrivastava

My name is Sakshi Srivastava, I am a student of class 12th writing since October 2018. I live in rewa madhya pradesh
Insta : the_inky_girl_

Swati Sudipta Barik

Hi, I'm Swati. I'm a biology student from cuttack. i write poems about human rights and love. You can contact me at swatibarik20@gmail.com
Insta : Barelyswati

Shubham Mudgil

An 18 year old extrovert who finds positivity in every moment of life. Lives careless and free to express and explore the world. Currently pursuing Political Science from Venky, DU.
Insta : hegemonised_by_passion

Adarsh Kumar Singh

Resting is as good as rusting
I love gothic writing.
Currently residing in GURGAON, just cleared with 12th, had a PCM combination.
Call me on 7835001106
Insta : adarsh_kumar.singh

Deepanksha Wadhwa

I am Deepanksha. I am from Gurgaon and I am currently in class 10 at DAVPS, Sector 14, Gurgaon. You can e-mail me at deepankshawadhwa@gmail.com or ping me at my whatsapp number 9911313344
Insta deep_waitforit_anksha

Samira Rahman

I'm Samira Rahman, a bong from Bangladesh. A newly appointed banker by days and doing whatever I like to do during the nights, just like Dr. Jeckyl and Mr. Hyde. Writing and poems and reading has become my solace now, and it keeps me on track.

Insta : samira.rahman666

Riya Adlakha

Hey I'm Riya Adlakha. I'm from gurgaon and currently pursuing journalism from Manipal University Jaipur. Nothing could be more powerful than words , so using my words as a sword is my type of a thing .
Insta :- riyaadlakha

Jayeesh Arora

Jayeesh Arora, a man who loves philosophy, romance and humour and a man who wishes to find the greater meaning.

Insta : jayesharora54

Navika Kaith

An eavesdropper who searches the world around her for inspiration and tries to translate its many stories into words and verse. Mostly a dreamer, other times a bibliophile. Currently pursuing her bachelors in English Literature from Sri Venkateswara College, University of Delhi.

Email ID - navikaith@gmail.com

Insta : navikakaith23

Pratistha Kharbanda

My name is Pratishtha Kharbanda. I am from Delhi and am majoring in English from Delhi University. My contact number is 8376941904 and email address is pratishtha.kharbanda@gmail.com

Insta : pratishthakharbanda_

Dev Chopra

It's suspicious when he doesn't talk in movie dialogues or doesn't hop around the room.
Dev Chopra, being married to drama is a poet with a very peculiar sense of thoughts.
A member of Natuve, the dramatics society of Shaheed Bhagat Singh College Morning may sometimes attend his lectures for the subjects offered in B.COM(H).
Insta : chanandelor_bong

Maanushi Sodhi

My name is Maanushi Sodhi. I have completed my schooling from DAVPS sec 14,ggn. I currently put up in Gurgaon.
Insta : memaanushi.sodhi

Yashashree Raghuwanshi

Name- SHREE (wants walls in her room to be made of novels). A mix of cultures from Gujrat, Mumbai, Delhi and now Bangalore!! Studied in a convent and then a public school!
Insta : __.s.h.r.e.e.__

Anant Seth

Anant Seth, from Bareilly, graduate in economics who likes to write in the dark after 3 am.
Instagram - anant20

Sukeerat Kaur Channi

Sukeerat shuttles between Delhi and Ludhiana as she figures out how to graduate. Writing poetry is as natural to her as winds to storm. In between scribbling phrases, incessant chatter and unread books, she likes to marvel at music, rain, sunlight and people. Appreciates if you laugh at her lame jokes.
Insta : afsaana_e_zindagi

Nitin Mukesh

I have completed my B.Sc from BHU in computer science and I look forward to improve my life ahead.

Manu Chauhan

An IITian currently pursuing B.Tech from IIT Madras, writing is a medium for me to express feelings, life's a web of entangled opportunities , seizing is what gets you the adventure, a jack of all trades with a nose for perfection
Insta : manu._.chauhan

Rachita Oberoi

20. I study in Sri Venkateswara College. I'm a singer/songwriter.
Insta: @rachitaoberoimusic

Kash Sheokand

19 year old medical student, going by the name of Kash Sheokand from a nothing town, currently in Mangalore. Read more of my work on TTT - https://terriblytinytales.com/user/kashsheokand , where I'm a featured writer.
Insta : snoutband11

SCAS

Hi. I'm SCAS. I've grown up in Delhi. I started writing almost six years back, and I still continue to write with all my heart. I'm a Computer Science Engineer in making, and hence, the meaning of ';' is different for me in both ways. Contact me through Instagram @_scas_ if you want. Love.
Insta : _scas_

Shivanshi Bhadhouria

I'm Shivanshi Bhadouria, I live in Delhi and I'm doing my bachelor's from DU. 9412115981
Insta: freakingoutsince1999

Archana Gajbinker

I'm Archana Gajbinkar from Hyderabad .
I'm 21 years old and persued Bachelor of Science and
Currently working for Deloitte as an Analyst .
Insta : archana_gajbinkar

Aayushi Verma

Hey, I'm a 19 year old MBBS student (2nd year) and my
name is Aayushi Verma. I live in Surat, Gujarat but
currently I'm studying in Wenzhou, China. Contact me at
aayushi.verma24@gmail.com.
Insta : shalalalala._.a

Deepanshi Rao

Hey, I'm Deepanshi. I'm somebody who fears oblivion so I paint it all in words. I'm a first year student at Lady Shri Ram College. I'm from Gurgaon, soon to be the city of dead. Save the Earth people.

Insta : Deepanshihihihi

Isha Adhikari

My name is Isha Adhikari, a high school senior year student. I'm from Bokaro Steel City, Jharkhand. I stay in Qr. no. 1047, Sector-12/F, B.S.City, Jharkhand, Pin code- 827012.

Insta :@ifeelsoisink_

Renita D'souza

 Hey, I'm Renita from Mangalore, and I've recently completed my BE in CSE. I've been writing ever since I could read, and I hope I get to keep doing it. Here's how you can contact me:
email: nita97lynn@gmail.com
Instagram: @the_unmasked_harlequin

Adhya Manocha

Adhya is a realist who dreams. A student from New Delhi, currently doing her schooling. She feels that metaphors and music can revive or ruin anything. A believer of art.

Insta : @coffee_and_carcasses

Aastha Takkar

Hola amigos!
You enter a poet's life as person ,but leave as a poem !
Aastha Takkar
Gurugram,Haryana
B.S.C(H)Botany ,Delhi university
Insta : aastha._.takkar

Parul Karn

Parul Karn, a born free rebel and a sucker for lyrics, poetry and stories. Currenty living in Mumbai, coz don't belong to no city and don't belong to no man. My sole purpose in this world is to find the absolute freedom.

I've just completed my B.Tech. and came back home.
Contact details: parulkarn42@gmail.com
Insta : parul_karn

Gaurav Chaudhary

A theatre fanatic, who leads various lives through different characters. A director, writer, actor who is currently doing Masters in Economis from DSE.

Anirudh Puranik

I am someone who always tries to make everyone around feel comfortable as soon as I enter the room.A guy who remembers all filmy dialogues as if they were a part of a conversation with my crush.

I know what to say at the right moment yet, I am not able to most of times.
I guess, I am someone who is still in search of who he actually is!
Insta id:anirudhpuranikk

Sambhav Chalana

A writer undermaking. I love all things aesthetic, beautiful and simple. Residing in Delhi but I hail from Malout in Punjab. Only write when I come across good prompts and find peace in soft melodies.

Tejashree Murugan

I'm Tejashree Murugan, from Chennai. I'm a third year student of Biotechnology at IIT Madras. You can reach me @earth2tj on Instagram.

Phalguni Jagadeesh

Myself Phalguni Jagadeesh. A budding writer with a passion to learn more and improve. A happy soul, finding peace through writing.
"There are many ways to achieve something in life and knowing the purpose of living and I got mine through words."
Insta : @phal_candy & @pjinklings

Shivangi Pahwa

Shivangi Pahwa
New Delhi
A weirdly sane science student who talks fandoms and aspires to live in peace. Writing since the age of nine, as far

as she remembers. Obsessed over Dead Poets Society and surviving on Nutella. Loves punching as much as she loves her friends. Thankyou, a poetic cardboard box. Instagram-@petalsfromhell

Pooja Trivedi Raval (SMIT)

I am Pooja raval. My pen name is SMIT. I know almost 16 Foreign languages . I am teaching those languages. I am from Ahmedabad.. i like to pen down my emotions frequently Insta : Poojahimadri

Dhiren Gor

I am Dhiren Gor. My pen name is Alfaz. I am from Ahmedabad. I am a corporate trainer. Sometimes I note down my emotions on paper.

Insta : Alfaz_dhiren_

Himani Raval

I am Himani Raval. My pen name is jindagi. I am from AHMEDABAD. I am going to turn 18 within few days.. i am a student of psychology and in 12th . Like to pen down my choices on paper...
Insta : Himani_2810

Manvi Sharma

Living life at edges and marking her own dream sequence, Manvi spills her heart on ink with stories that aren't clichéd. An English literature graduate, with a zest

to write her own vogue, Manvi has accomplished her own piece of phenomenal credit by getting published in three paperbacks, followed by a few online books and magazines. In love with the food of Delhi, Manvi is an explorer looking for experiences.
Insta : @manvi_poet

Harsh Bhardwaj

Harsh Bhardwaj, from Forbesganj (Bihar), 1st year English Honours student at SVC, 7250727022

Insta : harsh_bhardwaj04

Syeda Tahira Abidi

I am a person who loves to observe human behavior and psychology. I a am keen learner of culture and mythology, and love to spend my time reading novels.

Insta : syedatahiraabidi

Bhavya M Jain S

Hi,I'm Bhavya M Jain S ,my pen name is bhavv,I stay in Mysuru, Karnataka. I love writing,as it connects souls,deepens its roots & gives solace..

Rashi Soni

Rashi. A girl who has a thing for dried flowers and handwritten letters. Thinks that maps and directions are fascinating. Spent 20 years of life differentiating between citylights and stars. Hometown is Jalgaon and currently working up to add in to another engineer in the crowd.

Nil Dey

Born n brought up in Steel City Janshedpur Unsmart according to society Introvert according to Oxford Dictionary Kafir according to some Holy Books.

Chhavi Bambha

I talk politics, drink chai and find solace in books. Aspiring journalist. Part time student, full time procrastinator. I posses the capability to look pass the initial facade and I adorn what is presented to me in first instance.
Insta : chhavi_bahmba

Chetna Yadav

I'm Chetna Yadav - writer,artist and student. I am 19 years old and graduating in B.A (hons) English. I am trying to make a difference, I hope you are too.
Insta : chetna_5
Rahul Jena

I am a Poet, writer, and open mic poetry performer. Writing poems was always on my bucket list but I never knew I could write until I fell in love. I am pursuing Journalism and has a hardcore interest in the Media Industry
Insta : _.raaaahull._
Shreya Arora

Getting through life listening to Cigarettes after Sex and red wine. Apart from diligent note-making my hobbies include reading, writing, and talking to stars in the night. I wish to make a career in finance and my first and foremost love is dogs. Consider myself a unicorn trapped in a human body.

ABOUT REASONS AND LAUGHTER

Reasons and Laughter is a community which deals with providing services, compiling anthologies, organising competitions and Open Mics, found by Japneet Kaur.

Our main objective is to give a good platform to budding writers to help them grow, even to provide best services and giving wings to their dreams.

Email: ralservicess@gmail.com

Instagram: @reasons_and_laughter